Roar's About, Let's Go Out!

Hazel Reeves

Illustrated by Dave McTaggart

This is Roar,
the little dinosaur.

Roar is brave
and Roar is strong.
She often likes
to sing a song.

"Have we nearly
got there yet?
Is it dry
or is it wet?"

Roar likes beach huts,
little doors.
Stripy walls and
wooden floors.

"Five little beach huts
all in a row.
Take some pictures
I can show."

Roar likes trains
big and small.
Wheels and pistons
short and tall.

"Blow the whistle,
see the steam!
I am happy
with ice-cream."

Roar loves funfairs
with a friend.
Rides that take her
round the bend.

Roar likes animals,
different coats.
Rabbits, lambs,
and munching goats.

"Some are curly,
some are straight.
It's not lunch time —
you must wait!"

Roar is shopping
with her friend.
Both have money,
coins to spend.

"Toys and T-shirts,
what a lot!
Count my money,
what have I got?"

Roar, where are you?

Roar likes watching
lots of feet.
Different shoes
by every seat.

"I'm in headquarters
where I'll hide.
with my bag
right by my side."

Roar likes lunch time
in the corner.
Food all sorted
from her order.

"Juicy grapes,
crisps, bread roll.
Make neat islands
in my bowl."

Roar likes searching
for her friend.
Follows clues
until the end.

"I love this maze
with hedges straight.
I'll find my friend,
I won't be late."

Roar likes pushing
the garden trolley.
Hopes to buy
a frozen lolly.

"I've been busy,
I feel hot.
Ice-creams, lollies,
buy the lot!"

Roar likes washing
in a tub.
Spraying water,
then she'll scrub.

"Sprinkle, sprinkle,
on my head.
Is it nearly
time for bed?"

Roar likes camping
in the sunshine.
Thinks she'll go
inside for bedtime.

"Come on, Teddy,
that's enough.
Pack up all
my camping stuff."

Roar likes bedtime
with her light.
She feels safe
all through the night.

Granddad looks
around the door.
Sings a song
for little Roar.

"You go off out and look around.
Enjoy the places you have found.
You are an adventurous dinosaur.
I celebrate my little Roar."

Other Roar books available from LDA are:

Hello, Roar, Little Dinosaur (*intended to introduce Roar to children*)
Come on Roar, Let's Explore!
Roar's Creating, Let's Get Making!
Roar's In Shorts, Let's Play Sports!
Roar's Strumming, Let's Get Humming!

The rights of Hazel Reeves and Dave McTaggart to be identified as the authors of this work have been asserted by them in accordance with sections 77 and 78 of the Copyright, Designs and Patents Act 1988.

Roar's About, Let's Go Out!
ISBN: 978-1-85503-540-9
© Hazel Reeves and Dave McTaggart

LDA, Findel Education, Hyde Buildings, Ashton Road, Hyde, Cheshire, SK14 4SH